Clever Beatrice
and the Best Little Pony

Author's Note

In the old folklore of French-Canada, a lutin is most commonly known as an elf with surprising strength, which he uses to invade households and stables for good or ill, depending on how he is treated. A happy lutin will bring good fortune to a home, but if crossed, he can become a tricky rascal. Legends say that lutins travel by night and cannot bear to come face-to-face with humans, much less with clever little girls.

To Marlee
—M. W.
For Mom
—H. M. S.

Atheneum Books for Young Readers
An imprint of Simon & Schuster Children's Publishing Division
1230 Avenue of the Americas, New York, New York 10020
Text copyright © 2004 by Margaret Willey
Illustrations copyright © 2004 by Heather M. Solomon
All rights reserved, including the right of reproduction in whole or in part in any form.
Book design by Sonia Chaghatzbanian
The text for this book is set in Goudy.
The illustrations were rendered in watercolor, collage, acrylic, and oil paint.
Manufactured in China
First Edition
1 2 3 4 5 6 7 8 9 10

Library of Congress Cataloging-in-Publication Data
Willey, Margaret.
Clever Beatrice and the best little pony / Margaret Willey ; illustrated by Heather M. Solomon.—1st ed.
p.   cm.
Summary: Clever Beatrice seeks out Monsieur Le Pain, the village bread maker, to come up with a plan to protect her pony from the tiny bearded lutin that magically rides him every night.
ISBN 0-689-85339-4
[1. Folklore—Michigan. 2. Tall tales.] I. Solomon, Heather M., ill. II. Title.
PZ8 .1.W648Cn   2004
398.2   2003009520

Clever Beatrice
and the Best Little Pony

by Margaret Willey   illustrated by Heather M. Solomon

Atheneum Books for Young Readers
New York   London   Toronto   Sydney

In the far north woods, Beatrice was sipping her morning cocoa when her mother came in from the stable and said, "Someone-I-could-mention forgot to put her favorite pony to bed last night."

"Oh, Mother," said Beatrice. "I would never forget Trefflé! He is the best little pony in the whole north woods!"

"Ahem," her mother said. She waved for Beatrice to follow her, and together they walked to Trefflé's stable.

There, Beatrice could not believe her eyes. The pony's flanks were streaked with mud, his curly mane flecked with burrs. "I would never have left my pony in such a state!" she exclaimed. "Someone must have ridden him in the night, Mother! But who?"

"We will lock Trefflé's stable up extra carefully tonight," her mother said.

But the next morning it was exactly the same! The pony's mane was full of leaves and thistles, his flanks dirty, his eyes wild. Beatrice brought him a bucket of water, which he drank and drank as though he'd been running all night. "'Tis most strange," her mother said. "We must ask the village expert on things not easily explained."

"Who would that be?" wondered Beatrice.

"Why, Monsieur Le Pain, the new bread maker from Quebec."

So Beatrice put on her warmest sweater and walked down a twisting road, where a village had sprung up around the lumber camp near the river. The bread maker's shop had a bright sign over the door that read:

Fresh Bread & All Things Not Easily Explained

Inside, a man was kneading a mound of dough, an apron stretched across his broad chest. When he saw Beatrice in the doorway, he asked, "Who might you be, little brown eyes?"

"I am Beatrice," she said. "I live up the road with my mother."

"I have heard of you. Is it true that you won thirty gold coins from a rich giant?" asked Monsieur Le Pain.

"Oh yes," said Beatrice. "My mother used the gold to buy seeds for a garden, two goats, ten chickens, a strong horse, and a pony, just for me. Is it true you are an expert on things not easily explained?"

Monsieur Le Pain wiped his hands on his apron and came closer. "Do you need something explained, little Beatrice?" he asked. Beatrice told him about her pony. The bread maker listened, nodding his head. "Bedraggled and muddy in the morning?" he asked. "Burrs in the mane? Panting for water like a sick cat?" "Yes!" Beatrice agreed. "Can you explain it, sir?" "I don't like to tell you," he said, "but it does sound very much like a lutin. And lutins are trouble, to be sure. Little bearded men, smaller than you, who come from the old country.

"I myself have never seen one, but my uncle René from Repentigny once had a lutin in his stable, and the rascal wore out his prettiest pony in just two weeks."

"Oh, then I hope it is not a lutin!" Beatrice cried. "Is there a way to be sure?"

"I will put my great big brain to work on it for you," said Monsieur Le Pain. He began kneading again, kneading and frowning and punching the dough. Beatrice waited patiently, noticing that as Monsieur Le Pain moved around the table, he left a circle of footprints in the flour that had sifted to the floor.

"I have an idea, sir," she said. "What if I sprinkled flour on the floor in my pony's stable tonight and checked for lutin footprints in the morning?"

"Flour on the floor!" Monsieur Le Pain cried, lifting a finger. "Then watch for footprints, none bigger than a biscuit. Come back tomorrow and tell me what happens."

Beatrice walked home and told her mother what the bread maker had said. "A lutin!" Beatrice's mother scoffed. "Now I have heard everything."

Nevertheless, that night she helped Beatrice sprinkle flour onto the floor of Trefflé's stable. But the next morning Trefflé was again muddied and thirsty. Around him was a circle of tiny footprints. Beatrice's mother said, "Go and tell the bread maker!"

At the shop Monsieur Le Pain listened to Beatrice. "I don't like to tell you," he said, "but my uncle Louie from Lavaltrie once knew a man whose favorite pony was stolen by a lutin and never seen again!"

"Oh, I must save my pony!" Beatrice cried. "But how?"

"I will put my great big brain to work on it for you," Monsieur Le Pain said.

He began stacking bread pans and tins and carrying them down the stairs to his cellar. Up and down he went. "I have an idea, sir," Beatrice called from the top of the stairs. "Perhaps I should hide my pony in our cellar so that the lutin cannot find him."

"A pony in the cellar!" Monsieur Le Pain cried, coming back up the stairs. "So that the lutin cannot find him!"

Beatrice returned home and told her mother what they must do next. "A pony in the cellar!" her mother scoffed. "Now I have heard everything!" But that night she helped Beatrice move Trefflé into the cellar and put her mare in his place.

The next morning Beatrice awoke to the sound of her mother's cries from the kitchen. She ran from her bed and saw that someone had turned everything over—the kettle, the cauldron, the pots, and all the crockery!

"I must check the cellar!" Beatrice exclaimed. But when she went to put on her shoes, she found them full of pebbles! And when she reached for her sweater, she found that someone had sewn the sleeves shut, tight as pockets. Trefflé was sleeping safely in the cellar, but when she hurried to his stable, she found her mother's mare standing there looking very foolish—someone had arranged her mane into tight little braids, dozens and dozens of them, all down her back to the tip of her tail.

"Did you ever?" Beatrice's mother cried. "Go and tell the bread maker!"

Beatrice hurried into the village. "I don't like to tell you," said Monsieur Le Pain after hearing Beatrice's story, "but my uncle Baptiste from Beaupré once told me that lutins will make all kinds of trouble if they do not get their way."

"We have had quite enough of this lutin," Beatrice decided. "You must tell me how to get rid of him once and for all."

The bread maker was putting fresh loaves of bread into cloth sacks. "I will put my great big brain to work on it for you," he said. He put a dozen loaves into a sack and tied it shut with a cord, frowning and thinking.

"I have an idea," Beatrice said. "You could come to my pony's stable and catch the lutin in a bread sack."

"It is not an easy thing to catch a lutin!" Monsieur Le Pain protested. "I would have to wait until the middle of the night in your stable, where it would be very dark and cold."

"I will wait with you," Beatrice said. "And my mother will put blankets and fresh hay all around you so that you will be quite comfortable."

"Oh, but I am too busy, very busy! The lumberjacks need their bread, and there are many things not easily explained around here, to be sure."

"But, Monsieur Le Pain, sir, you said yourself that you have never seen a real lutin. Wouldn't it be the best not-easily-explained thing a person could ever see?"

Monsieur Le Pain took off his cap and shook the flour out of it, thinking. Finally he said to Beatrice, "Oh, very well, you. Run home now and tell your mother!"

When Beatrice told her mother that Monsieur Le Pain was coming to catch the lutin in a bread sack, her mother exclaimed, "Another wild idea from the bread maker!" But she put extra blankets in the stable and fresh hay on the floor.

As the sun went down, Beatrice and Monsieur Le Pain sat in the darkening stable. "I will cover myself up," Monsieur Le Pain said, picking up a blanket. "In the darkness the lutin will think that I am your pony, asleep in the hay. Then when he is beside me, I will sit up and look him straight in the eye. Like this!" He made his eyes huge and fierce for Beatrice. "A lutin cannot stand to be looked straight in the eye," he explained.

"Very good, sir," Beatrice said. Monsieur Le Pain gave a great yawn and lay down on the hay.

Beatrice settled onto a stool in the corner. Every so often she gave the bread maker's boot a sharp kick to help him stay awake. But it grew later and later, and the stable grew darker and darker, and all at once Beatrice realized that Monsieur Le Pain was snoring.

Suddenly she heard a soft scuffling coming from outside the stable. "Monsieur Le Pain!" she whispered. "I hear noises outside! What if it is the lutin?"

Then she heard a *scritch-scratch*, *scritch-scratch* at the window. It opened the slightest bit, and Beatrice saw a pair of tiny hands lift the heavy window. She gave Monsieur Le Pain the hardest kick that she could manage, but he only snored louder.

As Beatrice watched, a tiny man squeezed through the small space above the windowsill and into the stable. She saw that he was carrying a bridle. *To steal my Trefflé*, she thought.

She rushed from the shadows, grabbed the sack from beside the sleeping bread maker, and jumped in front of the lutin, looking him straight in the eye. "I am Beatrice," she cried. "And you cannot ride my pony ever again!" Then she threw the sack over the lutin's head.

The lutin began to struggle inside the sack and shriek, "Let me out! Let me out!"

Monsieur Le Pain awoke with a start, threw off his blanket, and shouted, "*Sacrebleu!* Do not let go of him, little Beatrice!"

"He is very strong, sir!" Beatrice cried. "Perhaps you could help me tie the sack!"

Monsieur Le Pain dug in his pocket for a cord while Beatrice held the sack. When it was tied at the top, they carried it together from the stable and put it into the back of Monsieur Le Pain's wagon.

The lutin kicked and shrieked all down the road until they came to the far side of the woods. There, Beatrice untied the sack and the lutin flew out, mad as a wet cat. In the moonlight they watched him run across the field, beard flying, until he disappeared among the trees. "There goes a real lutin, eh?" said Monsieur Le Pain.

"Are you quite sure that he will not come back?" Beatrice asked.

"He is too embarrassed to ever come back," Monsieur Le Pain said. "And I, for one, know how he feels."

On the ride back Beatrice fell asleep against Monsieur Le Pain. When they reached her house, the bread maker saw that Beatrice's mother had waited up for them. He lifted Beatrice from the wagon seat and carried her to the door. "It was a long night," he said. "Many things not easily explained."

"Did you catch the lutin?" Beatrice's mother asked, taking Beatrice into her arms.

"Oh, to be sure! The lutin will not trouble you again. She is a brave one, your Beatrice."

"Clever, too," said her mother. She thanked Monsieur Le Pain and carried Beatrice inside to her bed. Beatrice awoke just enough to ask, "Where is Trefflé?"

"In his very own stable," replied her mother, helping Beatrice into her nightshirt. "Sleeping like a baby, as you will soon be your own self."

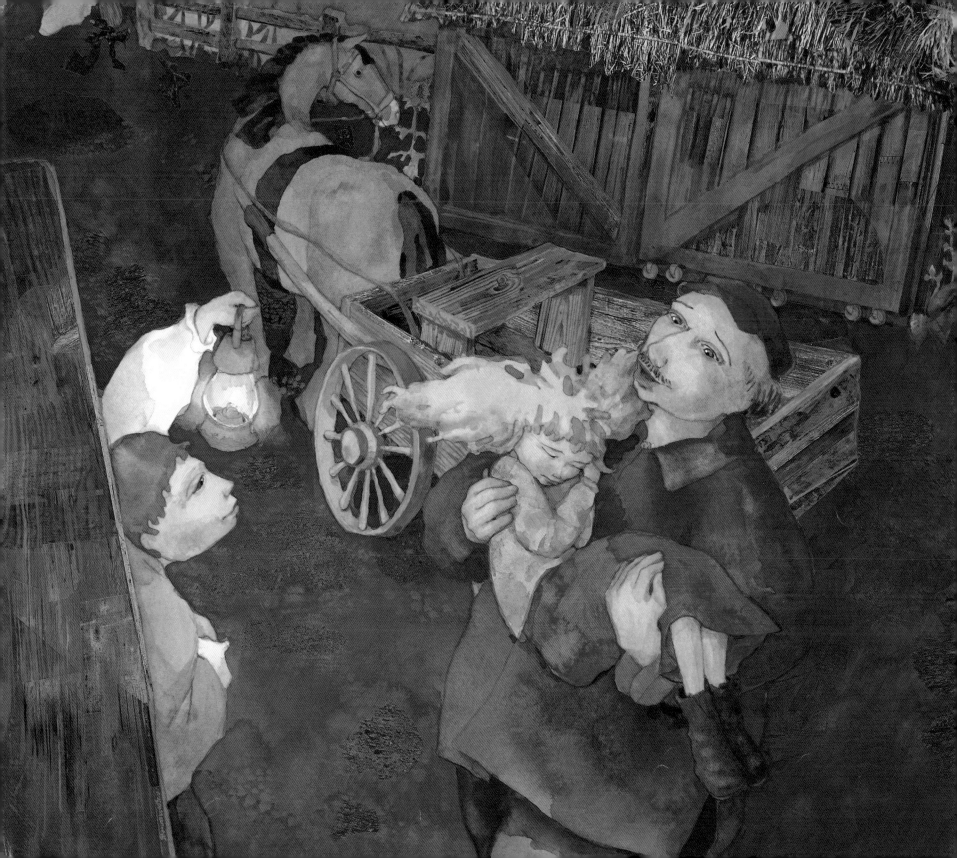

Beatrice closed her eyes and let her mother tuck her in. "Such a lucky pony," her mother said. "Tomorrow the most brave and clever girl in the whole north woods will ride him."

Beatrice smiled, hearing this, and was sound asleep again before her little smile was even finished.